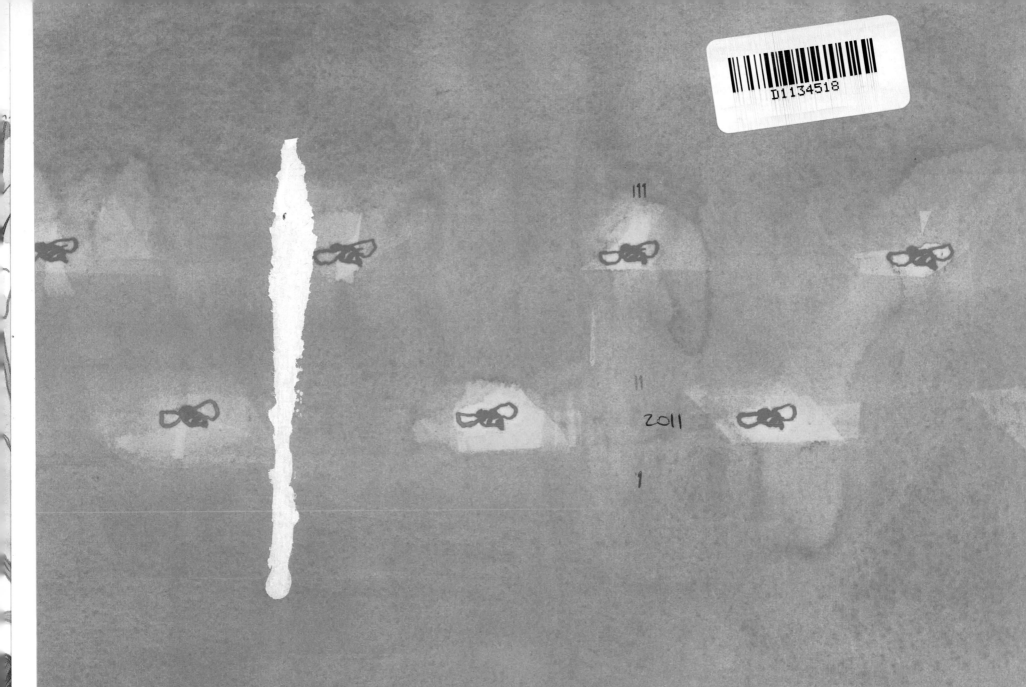

2011

No one ever came to Bear's house.

It had always been that way, and Bear

was quite sure he didn't like visitors.

He even had a sign:

One morning Bear heard a *tap, tap, tapping* on his front door.

When he opened it, there was a mouse, small and grey and bright-eyed.

"No visitors allowed," Bear said, pointing to the sign. "Go away."

He closed the door and went back to the business of making his breakfast.

He set out one cup and one spoon,

but when he opened the cupboard to get one bowl ...

there was the mouse! Small and grey and bright-eyed.

"I told you to leave!" cried Bear.

"Perhaps we could just have a drop of tea?" said the mouse.

"Out!" commanded Bear.

"Most sorry," said the mouse. "I'll be going now."

Bear showed him to the door and shut it firmly.

Then he went back to the business of making his breakfast.

But when he opened the bread drawer for one slice of bread ...

there was the mouse! Small and grey and bright-eyed.

"**Unbelievable!**" rumbled Bear.

"**Away with you! Clear off!**"

"I *do* like a bit of cheese," said the mouse.

Bear pointed a rigid claw towards the door.

"Right, then. Here I go. Farewell."

And the mouse whisked out of the door.

This time Bear shut the door very firmly and locked it tight.

He locked the windows too, for good measure.

Then, once again, he went back to the business of making his breakfast.

"Shall we light the fire?" asked the mouse.

"This is impossible! Intolerable! Insufferable!" cried Bear, shaking with anger and disbelief.

"Terribly sorry. Now you see me; now you don't. I am gone."
And the mouse looked very sorry indeed while he waited for
Bear to unbolt the door and let him out again.

This time, before he went back to the business of making his breakfast,

Bear shut the door very, very, VERY firmly, locked it,

boarded up the windows,

blocked the chimney,

and even put the plug in the bathtub.

Carefully, Bear set about the business of making his breakfast.

He opened the cupboard. No mouse. *Ahhhh!*

He opened the bread drawer. Nothing. *Phew!*

He opened the fridge. Mouse-free. *Yes, indeed!*

He lifted the lid from the kettle.

There was the mouse!

Small and grey and, well, you know the rest.

Bear fell to the floor.

"I give up," he blubbered. "You win. I am undone."

"So sorry," said the mouse. "But perhaps I could just have
a tiny bit of cheese and a cup of tea? And do you think we
could unblock the chimney and light a nice fire?"

Bear blew his nose with a loud honk.

"But *then* you must go," he sniffled. "No visitors allowed."

"You have my word," said the mouse.

Bear unboarded the windows,

unlocked the door,

unblocked the chimney

and took the plug out of the bath.

He brought out two plates of cheese and two teacups

and he lit a fire in the grate, for two sets of toes.

The mouse warmed his feet and nibbled and sipped, and Bear did too.

They sat for a long time. The clock on Bear's mantelpiece ticked loudly.

Bear cleared his throat.

The mouse looked most attentive. No one had ever been
most attentive to Bear.

"The fire is nice," Bear announced.

"Lovely," said the mouse.

No one had ever said Bear's fires were lovely.

"I can do a headstand," said Bear.

"Very impressive!" exclaimed the mouse.

Bear told a joke. The mouse laughed heartily. No one had ever laughed at Bear's jokes before. Bear began to think of another joke.

The mouse set down his teacup. Bear quickly lifted the teapot.

"There's plenty more," he said.

"So sorry," said the mouse. "Most kind, but I must be on my way."

"Really, you needn't go," said Bear.

"I am off," said the mouse, springing up from his chair.

"Wait," cried Bear.

But the mouse stepped out of the door.

"Toodle-oo," said the mouse.

"**Don't go!**" wailed Bear.

"But I gave you my word," said the mouse,

pointing at the "No Visitors" sign.

"Oh, *that*!" cried Bear, pulling down the sign and tearing it up.

"That's for salesmen. Not for friends."

"Not for friends?" asked the mouse, small and grey and bright-eyed.

Bear nodded. The mouse's bright eyes glowed brighter. Bear smiled.

"Do you like one lump of sugar or two?" said Bear, most politely.

"I like two," said the mouse. And Bear agreed.

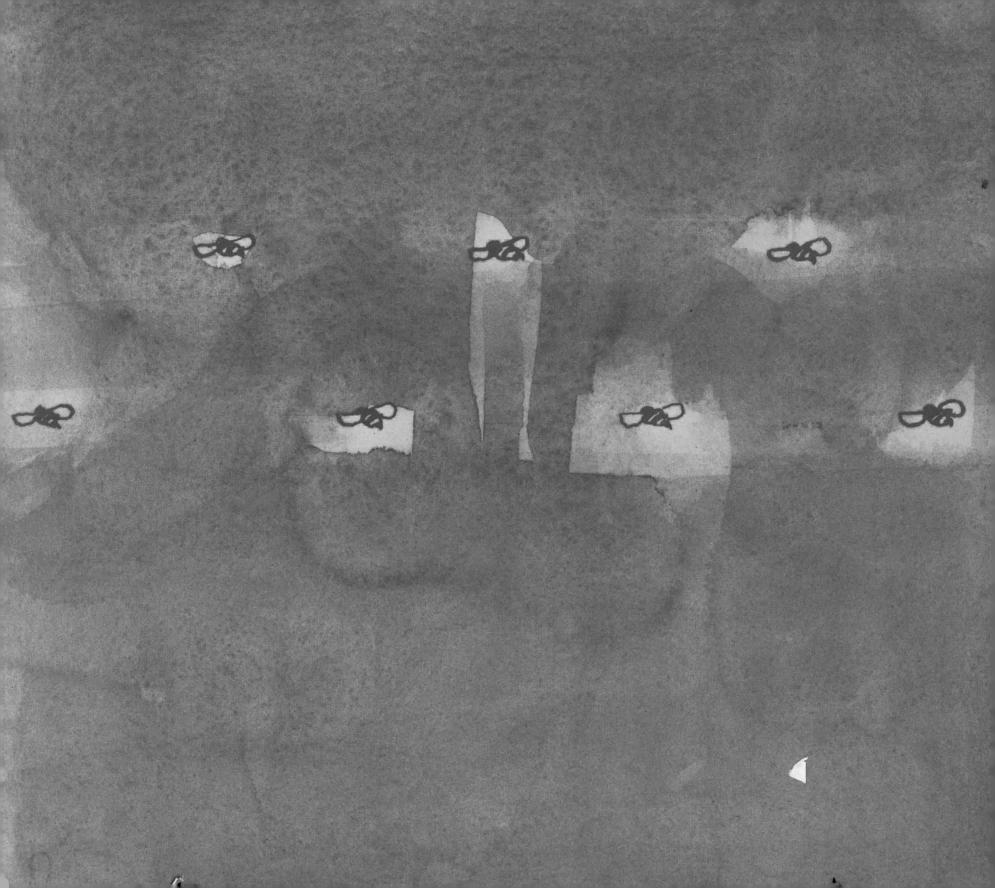